D0717462

90710 000 409 676

John Burningham

Mr Gumpy's Rhino

JONATHAN CAPE • LONDON

For Sudan the rhino

JONATHAN CAPE

UK | USA | Canada | Ireland | Australia
India | New Zealand | South Africa

Jonathan Cape is part of the Penguin Random House group of companies
whose addresses can be found at global.penguinrandomhouse.com.

www.penguin.co.uk www.puffin.co.uk www.ladybird.co.uk

First published 2019
001

Printed in China
A CIP catalogue record for this book is available from the British Library

ISBN: 978-0-857-55201-3

All correspondence to:
Jonathan Cape, Penguin Random House Children's
80 Strand, London WC2R 0RL

Mr Gumpy was travelling in Africa . . .

. . . when he came across something very sad.

There was a baby rhinoceros who had lost his mother and father. Somebody had taken their horns away.

Mr Gumpy knew that the baby rhino needed milk. Mr Gumpy had *some* milk, but not enough for a rhino.

He managed to buy more milk from some Bedouins who lived in the desert. But it wasn't enough.

Mr Gumpy drove through the night because it was so hot in the day. “I am going to call you Charlie,” he said to the rhino.

Mr Gumpy and Charlie arrived at the port and drove their car on to the boat.

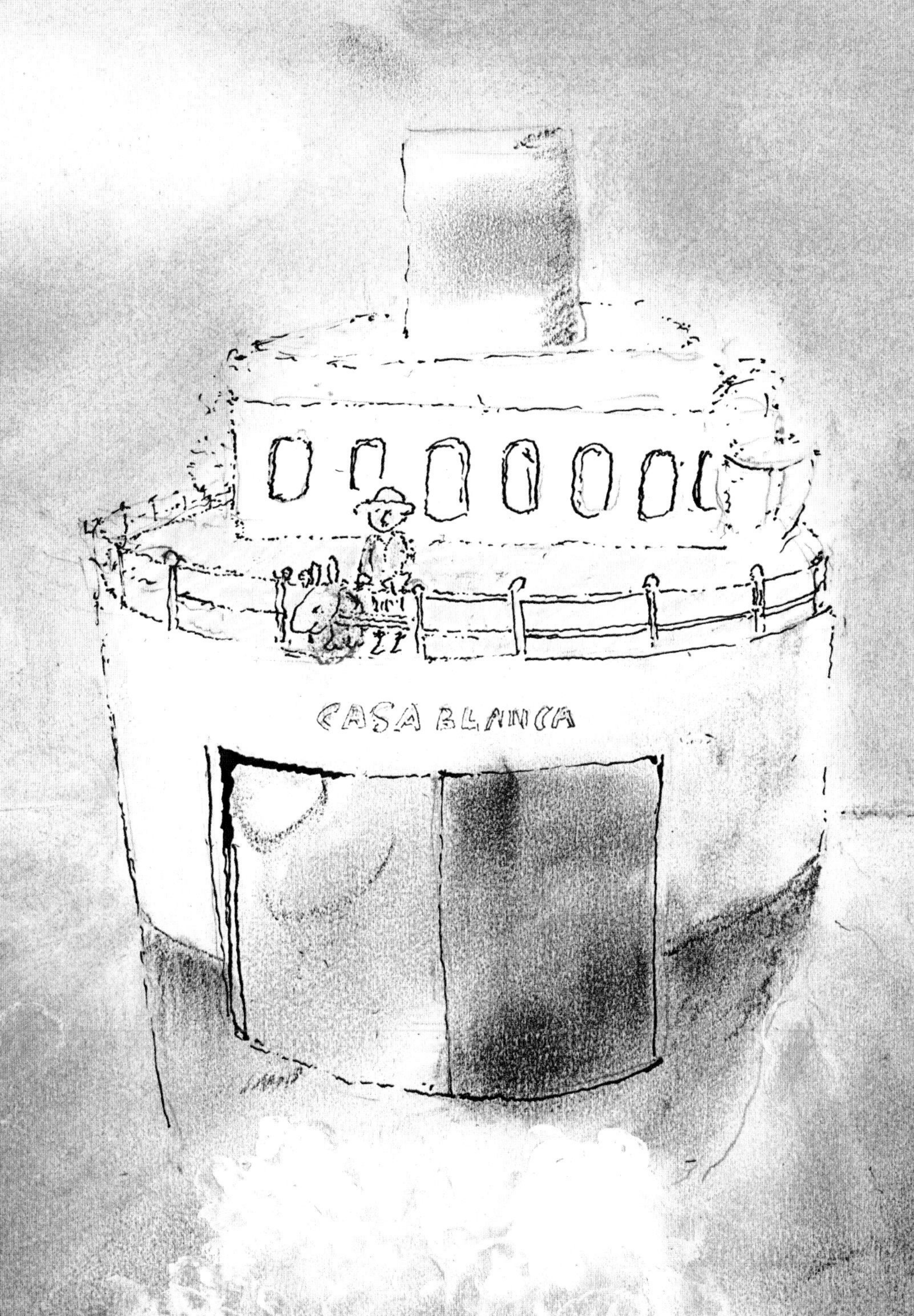
CASA BLANCA

They were both very tired
and soon fell asleep.

The next morning Mr Gumpy was able to get lots of milk and bunches of lettuce for the rhino.

At last Mr Gumpy was back in his own house. Already he was finding it difficult to get enough food for Charlie, who was growing fast.

Mr Gumpy decided to take Charlie to see the children at the school. He told the teacher and the children about needing more food for Charlie.

"That rhino should be working for the local council eating all the grass and leaves at the side of the road," said a boy. Mr Gumpy thought that was a good idea.

The council gave Charlie a special jacket to wear and he started work at the side of the road. He loved his jacket and eating the grass. They also gave him a sign that said:

TAKE CARE. RHINO AT WORK.

Every summer term the children went to the seaside for a trip on a boat. They all looked forward to this. But this year the traffic was terrible and their bus got stuck. They thought that they were going to miss the boat.

"Charlie could take us if only he were here."
"Look, Charlie is coming!"

All the children got out of the bus and climbed onto Charlie.

Charlie didn't need a road. He charged through the hedges in a straight line towards the sea.

They got to the beach, and could see that the boat had already left. But Charlie did not stop.

Charlie went into the water and got to the boat.
The children were able to climb aboard.

"Hooray for Charlie!"

UDG

Charlie is a good rhino. He likes his work and living with Mr Gumpy.

Sometimes when he feels a bit naughty,

he rolls in the mud . . .

. . . or – when nobody's looking – he eats the flowers.